Hi. My name is Sally, and I wear a
safe from germs. Germs can mak
My mask has smiley faces. Do you know why?

I'm smiling behind my mask!
Can you guess who's behind
each mask?

A mask with hearts?

...it's my mom. She loves me lots!

A mask with bows...

...it's my sister. She likes to wear a crown.

Guess who wears a mask with baseballs?

It's my dad!

The mask with the banana...

...it's my Nana.

And who's behind this mask?

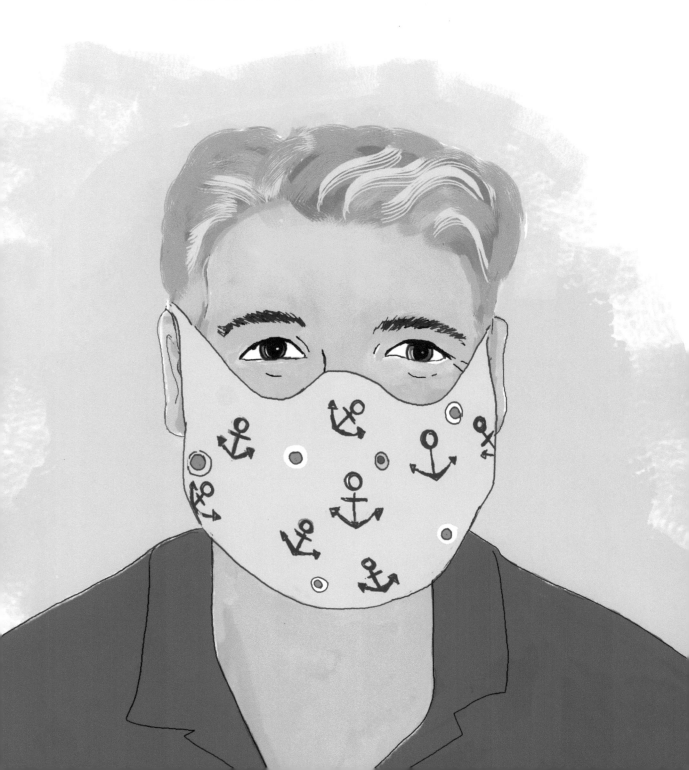

It's Pop-pop!

Other people wear masks, too.
Donuts and cake on a mask?

It's the grocery store clerk.
He puts food on our shelves.

Who's behind this mask?

It's my teacher!

Who wears a mask and shield?

A doctor, nurse, and...

...anyone who sees a lot of people.
They must be extra careful.

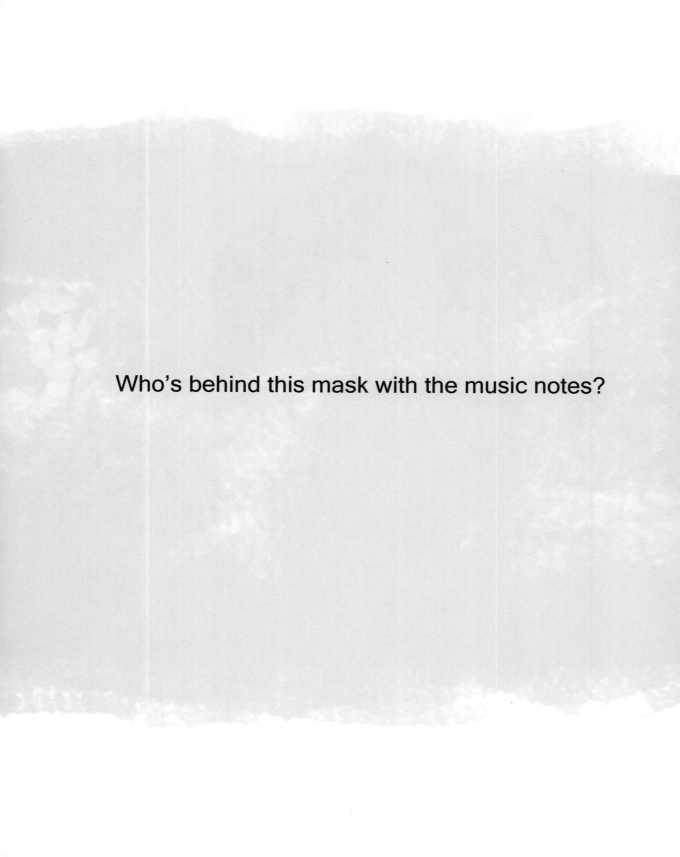

Who's behind this mask with the music notes?

My friend Ben.

A mask with bones?!?

NO...

Dogs don't wear masks!

What type of mask do you like to wear?

Dedicated to Steve with all my love.

www.konkol.com

ISBN: 978-1-7359196-0-7

The artist used pen and ink and added color digitally to create the illustrations for this book.

First Edition. November 2020, 32 pages, 7.5" x 9.25", POD

CPSIA information can be obtained
at www.ICGtesting.com
Printed in the USA
LVHW052325090921
697439LV00002B/42